Anonymous

Napoleon's Oraculum and Dream Book

Containing the great oracle of human destiny

Anonymous

Napoleon's Oraculum and Dream Book
Containing the great oracle of human destiny

ISBN/EAN: 9783337382919

Printed in Europe, USA, Canada, Australia, Japan

Cover: Foto ©Andreas Hilbeck / pixelio.de

More available books at **www.hansebooks.com**

NAPOLEON'S ORACULUM

AND

DREAM BOOK.

CONTAINING

The Great Oracle of Human Destiny.

ALSO

THE TRUE MEANING OF ALMOST ANY KIND OF DREAMS,

TOGETHER WITH

Charms, Ceremonies, and Curious Games of Cards.

A COMPLETE BOOK,

NEW YORK:

FRANK TOUSEY, Publisher,

34 AND 36 NORTH MOORE STREET.

NAPOLEON'S ORACULUM

AND

DREAM BOOK.

NAPOLEON'S ORACULUM; or, BOOK OF FATE

THE ORACULUM IS GIFTED WITH EVERY REQUISITE VARIETY OF
RESPONSE TO THE FOLLOWING QUESTIONS:

1. Shall I obtain my wish?
2. Shall I have success in my undertakings?
3. Shall I gain or lose in my cause?
4. Shall I have to live in foreign parts?
5. Will the stranger return?
6. Shall I recover my property?
7. Will my friend be true?
8. Shall I have to travel?
9. Does the person love and regard me?
10. Will the marriage be prosperous?
11. What sort of a wife or husband, shall I have?
12. Will she have a son or daughter?
13. Will the patient recover?
14. Will the prisoner be released?
15. Shall I be lucky or unlucky?
16. What does my dream signify?

HOW TO WORK THE ORACULUM.

Make marks in four lines, one under another, in the following manner, making more or less in each line, according to your

Then reckon the number of marks in each line, and, if it be *odd*, mark down one dot; if *even*, two dots. If there be more than nine marks, reckon the surplus ones over that number only, viz.:

The number of marks in the first line of the foregoing are *odd;* therefore make one mark, thus . . . . . . *

In the second, *even*, so make two, thus . . . . * *

In the third, *odd* again, make one mark only . . . *

In the fourth, *even* again, two marks . . . . * :

TO OBTAIN THE ANSWER.

You must refer to THE ORACULUM, at the top of which you will find a row of dots similar to those you have produced, and a column of figures corresponding with those prefixed to the questions; guide your eye down the column at the top of which you find the dots resembling your own, till you come to the letter on a line with the number of the question you are trying, then refer to the page having that letter at the top, and, on a line with the dots which are similar to your own, you will find your *answer.*

The following are unlucky days, on which none of the questions should be worked, or any enterprise undertaken: Jan. 1, 2, 4, 6, 10, 20, 22; Feb. 6, 17, 28; March 24, 26; April 10, 27, 28; May 7, 8; June 27; July 17, 21; Aug. 20, 22; Sept. 5, 30; Oct. 6; Nov. 3, 29; Dec. 6, 10, 15.

** It is not right to try a question twice in one day.

ORACULUM.

Numb.	QUESTIONS.																
1	Shall I obtain my wish?	A	B	C	D	E	F	G	H	I	K	L	M	N	O	P	Q
2	Shall I have success in my undertakings?	B	C	D	E	F	G	H	I	K	L	M	N	O	P	Q	A
3	Shall I gain or lose in my cause?	C	D	E	F	G	H	I	K	L	M	N	O	P	Q	A	B
4	Shall I have to live in foreign parts?	D	E	F	G	H	I	K	L	M	N	O	P	Q	A	B	C
5	Will the stranger return from abroad?	E	F	G	H	I	K	L	M	N	O	P	Q	A	B	C	D
6	Shall I recover my property stolen?	F	G	H	I	K	L	M	N	O	P	Q	A	B	C	D	E
7	Will my friend be true in his dealings?	G	H	I	K	L	M	N	O	P	Q	A	B	C	D	E	F
8	Shall I have to travel?	H	I	K	L	M	N	O	P	Q	A	B	C	D	E	F	G
9	Does the person love and regard me?	I	K	L	M	N	O	P	Q	A	B	C	D	E	F	G	H
10	Will the marriage be prosperous?	K	L	M	N	O	P	Q	A	B	C	D	E	F	G	H	I
11	What sort of wife or husb. shall I have?	L	M	N	O	P	Q	A	B	C	D	E	F	G	H	I	K
12	Will she have a son or a daughter?	M	N	O	P	Q	A	B	C	D	E	F	G	H	I	K	L
13	Will the patient recover from his illness?	N	O	P	Q	A	B	C	D	E	F	G	H	I	K	L	M
14	Will the prisoner be released?	O	P	Q	A	B	C	D	E	F	G	H	I	K	L	M	N
15	Shall I be lucky or unlucky this day?	P	Q	A	B	C	D	E	F	G	H	I	K	L	M	N	O
16	What does my dream signify?	Q	A	B	C	D	E	F	G	H	I	K	L	M	N	O	P

A

✸✸✸✸	What you wish for, you will shortly OBTAIN.
✸✸ ✸✸	Signifies trouble and sorrow.
✸✸ ✸✸	Be very cautious what you do THIS day, lest trouble befall you.
✸✸ ✸✸	The prisoner DIES, and is regretted by his friends.
✸✸ ✸✸	Life will be spared THIS time, to prepare for death.
✸✸ ✸✸	A very handsome daughter, but a PAINFUL one.
✸✸ ✸✸	You will have a virtuous woman or man, for your wife or husband.
✸✸ ✸✸	If you marry this person, you will have enemies where you little expect.
✸✸ ✸✸	You had better decline THIS love, for it is neither constant nor true.
✸✸ ✸✸	DECLINE your travels, for they will not be to your advantage.
✸✸ ✸✸	There is a true and sincere friendship between you BOTH.
✸✸ ✸✸	You will NOT recover the stolen property.
✸✸ ✸✸	The stranger WILL, with joy, soon return.
✸✸ ✸✸	You will NOT remove from where you are at present.
✸✸ ✸✸	Providence WILL support you in a good cause.
✸✸ ✸✸	You are NOT lucky.

B

	The luck that is ordained for you will be coveted by others.
	Whatever your desires are, for the present decline them.
	Signifies a favor or kindness from some person.
	There ARE enemies who would defraud and render you unhappy.
	With great difficulty he will obtain pardon or release again.
	The patient should be prepared to LEAVE this world.
	She will have a SON, who will be learned and wise.
	A RICH partner is ordained for you.
	By THIS marriage you will have great luck and prosperity.
	THIS love comes from an upright and sincere heart.
	A higher Power WILL surely travel with you, and bless you.
	Beware of friends who are false and deceitful.
	You WILL recover your property—unexpectedly.
	Love prevents his return home at present.
	Your stay is NOT here; be therefore prepared for a change.
	You will have NO GAIN; therefore be wise and careful.

C

	With the blessing of God, you WILL have great gain.
	Very unlucky indeed—pray for assistance.
	If your desires are NOT extravagant, they will be granted.
	Signifies peace and plenty between friends.
	Be well prepared THIS day, or you may meet with trouble.
	The prisoner WILL find it difficult to obtain his pardon or release.
	The patient WILL YET enjoy health and prosperity.
	She WILL have a daughter, and will require attention.
	The person has NOT a great fortune, but is in middling circumstances.
	Decline THIS marriage, or else you may be sorry.
	Decline a courtship which MAY be your destruction.
	Your travels are IN VAIN; you had better stay at home.
	You MAY depend on a true and sincere friendship.
	You must NOT expect to regain that which you have lost.
	SICKNESS prevents the traveler from seeing you.
	It WILL be your fate to stay where you now are.

D

⋮	You WILL obtain a great fortune in another country.
⋮	By venturing freely, you WILL certainly gain doubly.
⋮	A higher Power WILL change your misfortune into success and happiness.
⋮	Alter your intentions, or else you MAY meet poverty and distress.
⋮	Signifies you have many impediments in accomplishing your pursuits.
⋮	Whatever may possess your inclinations this day, abandon them.
⋮	The prisoner WILL get free again this time.
⋮	The patient's illness WILL be lingering and doubtful.
⋮	She will have a dutiful and handsome son.
⋮	The person will be LOW in circumstances, but honest-hearted.
⋮	A marriage which WILL ADD to your welfare and prosperity.
⋮	You love a person who does not speak well of you.
⋮	Your travels WILL be prosperous, if guided by prudence.
⋮	He means NOT what he says, for his heart is false.
⋮	With some trouble and expense, you may regain your property.
⋮	You must NOT expect to see the stranger again.

E

	The stranger WILL not return as soon as you expect.
	Remain among your friends, and you will do well.
	You will hereafter GAIN what you seek.
	You have NO LUCK—pray, and strive honestly.
	You will obtain your wishes by means of a friend.
	Signifies you have enemies who will endeavor to ruin you.
	Beware—an enemy is endeavoring to bring you to strife and misfortune.
	The prisoner's sorrow and anxiety are great, and his release uncertain.
	The patient WILL soon recover—there is no danger.
	She will have a daughter, who will be honored and respected.
	Your partner WILL be fond of liquor, and will debase himself thereby.
	This marriage will bring you to poverty, be therefore discreet.
	Their love is false to you, and true to others.
	DECLINE your travels for the present, for they will be dangerous.
	THIS person is serious and true, and deserves to be respected.
	You will not recover the property you have lost.

	By persevering you WILL recover your property again.
	It is out of the stranger's power to return.
	You will GAIN, and be successful in foreign parts.
	A great fortune is ordained for you; wait patiently.
	There is great hindrance to your success at present.
	Your wishes are in VAIN at present.
	Signifies there are sorrow and danger before you.
	THIS day is unlucky; therefore alter your intention.
	The prisoner will be restored to liberty and freedom.
	The patient's recovery is doubtful.
	She will have a fine BOY.
	A worthy person, and a fine fortune.
	Your intentions would destroy your rest and peace.
	THIS love is true and constant; forsake it not.
	PROCEED on your journey, and you will not have cause to repent it.
	If you trust THIS friend, you may have cause for sorrow.

G

	This friend exceeds all others in every respect.
	You must bear your loss with fortitude.
	The stranger will return unexpectedly.
	Remain at HOME with your friends, and you will escape misfortunes.
	You will meet no GAIN in your pursuits.
	Heaven will bestow its blessings on you.
	No.
	Signifies that you will shortly be out of the POWER of your enemies.
	ILL-LUCK awaits you—it will be difficult for you to escape it.
	The prisoner will be RELEASED by death only.
	By the blessing of God, the patient WILL recover.
	A daughter, but of a very sickly constitution.
	You will get an honest, young, and handsome partner.
	Decline this marriage, else it may be to your sorrow.
	Avoid this love.
	Prepare for a short journey; you will be recalled by unexpected events.

H

‡	Commence your travels, and they will go on as you could wish.
‡	Your pretended friend hates you secretly.
‡	Your hopes to recover your property are vain.
‡	A certain affair prevents the stranger's return immediately.
‡	Your fortune you will find in abundance abroad.
‡	Decline the pursuit, and you will do well.
‡	Your expectations are vain—you will not succeed.
‡	You will obtain what you wish for.
‡	Signifies that on this day your fortune will change for the better.
‡	Cheer up your spirits, your luck is at hand.
‡	After LONG imprisonment, he will be released.
‡	The patient will be relieved from sickness.
‡	She will have a healthy SON.
‡	You will be married to your equal in a short time.
‡	If you wish to be happy, do not marry this person.
‡	This love is from the heart, and will continue until death.

I

✱	The love is great, but will cause great jealousy.
✱✱	It will be in vain for you to travel.
✱✱	Your friend will be as sincere as you could wish him to be.
✱✱	You will recover the stolen property through a cunning person.
✱✱	The traveler will soon return with joy.
✱✱	You will not be prosperous or fortunate in foreign parts.
✱✱	Place your trust in God, who is the disposer of happiness.
✱✱	Your fortune will shortly be changed into misfortune.
✱✱	You will succeed as you desire.
✱✱	Signifies that the misfortune which threatens will be prevented.
✱✱	Beware of your enemies, who seek to do you harm.
✱✱	After a short time, your anxiety for the prisoner will cease.
✱✱	God will give the patient health and strength again.
✱✱	She will have a very fine daughter.
✱✱	You will marry a person with whom you will have little comfort.
✱✱	The marriage will not answer your expectations.

K

	After much misfortune, you will be comfortable and happy.
	A sincere love from an upright heart.
	You will be prosperous in your journey. .
	Do not RELY on the friendship of this person.
	The property is lost for EVER; but the thief will be punished.
	The traveler will be absent some considerable time.
	You will meet luck and happiness in a foreign country.
	You will not have any success for the present.
	You will succeed in your undertaking.
	Change your intentions, and you will do well.
	Signifies that there are rogues at hand.
	Be reconciled, your circumstances will shortly mend.
	The prisoner will be released.
	The patient will depart this life.
	She will have a son.
	It will be difficult for you to get a partner.

L

⁝	You will get a very handsome person for your partner.
⁞⁞	Various misfortunes will attend this marriage.
⁝⁝	This love is whimsical and changeable.
⁞⁞	You will be unlucky in your travels.
⁞⁞	This person's love is just and true. You may rely on it.
⁞⁞	You will lose, but the thief will suffer most.
⁞⁞	The stranger will soon return with plenty.
⁞⁞	If you remain at home, you will have success.
⁞⁞	Your gain will be trivial.
⁞⁞	You will meet sorrow and trouble.
⁞⁞	You will succeed according to your wishes.
⁞⁞	Signifies that you will get money.
⁞⁞	In spite of enemies, you will do well.
⁞⁞	The prisoner will pass many days in confinement.
⁞⁞	The patient will recover.
⁞⁞	She will have a daughter.

M

⁂	She will have a son, who will gain wealth and honor.
⁂	You will get a partner with great undertakings and much money.
⁂	The marriage will be prosperous.
⁂	She, or He, wishes to be yours this moment.
⁂	Your journey will prove to your advantage.
⁂	Place no great trust in that person.
⁂	You will find your property at a certain time.
⁂	The traveler's return is rendered doubtful by his conduct.
⁂	You will succeed as you desire in foreign parts.
⁂	Expect no gain; it will be in vain.
⁂	You will have more LUCK than you expect.
⁂	Whatever your desires are, you will speedily obtain them.
⁂	Signifies you will be asked to a wedding.
⁂	You will have no occasion to complain of ill-luck.
⁂	Some one will pity and release the prisoner.
⁂	The patient's recovery is unlikely.

N

✳	The patient will recover, but his days are short.
✳	She will have a daughter.
✳	You will marry into a very respectable family.
✳	By this marriage you will gain nothing.
✳	Await the time and you will find the love great.
✳	Venture not from home.
✳	This person is a sincere friend.
✳	You will never recover the theft.
✳	The stranger will return, but not quickly.
✳	When abroad, keep from evil women or they will do you harm.
✳	You will soon gain what you little expect.
✳	You will have great success.
✳	Rejoice ever at that which is ordained for you.
✳	Signifies that sorrow will depart, and joy will return.
✳	Your luck is in blossom ; it will soon be at hand.
✳	Death may end the imprisonment.

O

	The prisoner will be released with joy.
	The patient's recovery is doubtful.
	She will have a son, who will live to a great age.
	You will get a virtuous partner.
	Delay not this marriage—you will meet much happiness.
	None loves you better in this world.
	You may proceed with confidence.
	Not a friend, but a secret enemy.
	You will soon recover what is stolen.
	The stranger will not return again.
	A foreign woman will greatly enhance your fortune.
	You will be cheated out of your gain.
	Your misfortunes will vanish and you will be happy.
	Your hope is in vain—fortune shuns you at present.
	That you will soon hear agreeable news.
	There are misfortunes lurking about you.

P

	This day brings you an increase of happiness.
	The prisoner will quit the power of his enemies.
	The patient will recover and live long.
	She will have two daughters.
	A rich young person will be your partner.
	Hasten your marriage--it will bring you much happiness.
	The person loves you sincerely.
	You will not prosper from home.
	This friend is more valuable than gold.
	You will NEVER receive your goods.
	He is dangerously ill, and cannot yet return.
	Depend upon your own industry, and remain at home.
	Be joyful, for future prosperity is ordained for you.
	Depend not too much on your good luck.
	What you wish will be granted to you.
	That you should be very careful this day, lest any accident befall you.

Q

	Signifies much joy and happiness between friends.
	This day is not very lucky, but rather the reverse.
	He will yet come to honor, although he now suffers.
	Recovery is doubtful; therefore be prepared for the worst.
	She will have a son who will prove forward.
	A rich partner, but a bad temper.
	By wedding this person you insure your happiness.
	The person has great love for you, but wishes to conceal it.
	You may proceed on your journey without fear.
	Trust him not; he is inconstant and deceitful.
	In a very singular manner you will recover your property.
	The stranger will return very soon.
	You will dwell abroad in comfort and happiness.
	If you will deal fairly you will surely prosper.
	You will yet live in splendor and plenty.
	Make yourself contented with your PRESENT fortune.

THE TRUE MEANING OF DREAMS.

ACQUAINTANCE. To dream that you fight with them, signifies distraction, especially if the person so dreaming be sick.

ADULTERY. To dream of the commission of this sin forebodes great troubles and misfortunes—if you are in love, you will certainly fail in marrying the object of your wishes—if you have a law-suit, it will certainly go against you, by the treachery of those who pretended to be your friends—if you are in business, some heavy loss will happen to you. Such a dream announces that you are in great danger of losing your liberty—and if you are about to take a voyage by sea, omit it for the present, for you will never reach the destined port. To dream you were tempted to commit this crime, and that you resisted it, is a happy omen—everything will flourish with you —be sure it is a good time to begin trade after such a dream. If you have a law-suit all will go in your favor, with credit to yourself and confusion in your opponents; if you are about to undertake a long journey, it will be pleasant and successful to your object; if you are going to sea you will have an agreeable voyage, fine weather, and a quick arrival at the port of destination; if you are in love, press the object of your wishes, for they will be gratified.

ALMS. To dream that they are begged of you, and you deny to give them, shows want and misery to the dreamer; but to dream that you give them freely, is a sign of great joy, and of long life to the dreamer.

ALTAR. To dream you see an altar, signifies consolation and joy. To adorn an altar is a sign of a speedy marriage.

ANCHOR. To dream you see one, signifies great assurance and certain hope.

ANGER. To dream that you have been provoked to anger, shows that you have many powerful enemies.

ANTS. To dream of them, betokens an earthly, covetous mind; and, as they live under the earth, to dream often of them, shows the dreamer not to be long lived. To see ants with wings, shows a dangerous voyage, or other ill accident. To dream you see common ants, which are diligent and industrious in providing their food, is good for farmers, because they signify fertility; for where there is no grain, you will find no ants. To such as live upon the public, and reap profits by many, they are very good; and to such as are sick, if they dream they come near the body; for they are industrious, and cease not to labor, which is proper to such as live; but if they dream that ants range about their bodies, it is a token of death; because they are inhabitants of earth, and are cold and black.

ANGELS. To dream you see angels in your sleep, is a sure sign that some one is near you; therefore be mindful of the rest of your dream, for it will come to pass pretty accurately; should you only dream you see nothing but an angel, or angels, then it denotes health, prosperity, and much happiness, with many children, who will all turn out good. If a woman with child dreams of them, she will have a good time, and perhaps twins; if you are in love, nothing can be more favorable, and all your undertakings will prosper, and be advantageous to you.

APPARITIONS. To dream you see a ghost, hobgoblin, specter, and such kind of things, is of a very unfortunate nature: they denote vexation and disappointment; if you are in love, it is a certain sign of your not being beloved in return, that the object of your affections either hates you or despises you; depend upon it some one is about to deceive you, and that you are in the habit of friendship with one who is your most inveterate enemy; do not undertake a journey just at this time, for it will be unfortunate to you; and be careful of contracting debts, for such a dream forebodes great trouble through some one to whom you shall owe money.

APPLES. To dream you see apple-trees, and eat sweet and ripe apples, denotes joy, pleasure, and recreation, especially to virgins: but sour apples signify contention and sedition.

ARTICHOKES. (See Vegetables.)

ASPARAGUS. (See Vegetables.)

ASHES. Foretell a great misfortune is at hand.

ASPS. To dream of asps, denotes that you will become extremely rich, and have great quantities of money by you: if you are in love, it imports that your love will be returned, and that your sweetheart will become through your means extremely wealthy.

ASS. The ass in dreams denotes a good servant or slave, that is profitable to his master; it also indicates a foolish and ignorant person. To dream you see an ass, is a sign of malice. To see an ass sitting on his crupper, denotes laboriousness. To dream you hear an ass bray, shows you shall meet with some loss. To dream of asses bearing charge, strong and obedient, is good for friendship and company, and signifies the wife's companion or friend, being not proud above their estate, or fierce, but gentle and very obedient; they are also good in affairs and enterprises. To see an ass run, denotes misfortune, especially to a man that is sick.

AWAKENING. To dream you awake from a sleep signifies you will inspire love with the one you wish. To awaken another person, shows that you will have a happy end to all sorrow.

AUTHORITY. It is good always for a rich man to think or dream he is in authority.

BACK. To dream you see your back, betokens some unhappiness; for the back and all the hinder parts signify old age. To dream a man's back is broken, hurt, or scabby, shows his enemies will get the better of him, and that he will be scoffed at. To dream of the back-bone, indicates health and joy, and that he will take delight in his wife and children.

BAGPIPES. (See Plays.) To dream that you play upon them, denotes trouble, contention, and being overthrown at law.

BALL. To dream you go to a ball signifies you will be unfortunate in all your undertakings. Do not go into any speculations after such a dream. To dream you are playing at ball, denotes success in business.

BANQUETS. To dream of banquets is very good and prosperous, and promises great preferment.

BARN. To dream you see a barn stored with corn, shows that you shall marry a rich wife, overthrow your adversary at law, inherit land, or grow rich by trading. To seen an empty barn betokens disappointment. On fire, a sudden gain.

BAT. (See Owl.)

BAKING. (See Brewing.)

BATH. To dream one sees a bath, is a sign of affliction or grief. If a person dreams he goes into or sees himself in a bath, and that he finds it too hot, he will be troubled and afflicted by those that belong to his family. If one dreams he has only pulled off his clothes, without going into the bath, he will have some disturbance, but of no long continuance. If one dreams he goes into an extremely cold bath, the same signification is to be given of it as when it is too hot. But if it be temperate, and as it ought to be, it is a good dream, presaging prosperity, joy and health.

BAY-TREE. To dream of the bay-tree, denotes a rich and fair wife; and also ill success of affairs, because it is bitter; but it is good for physicians, poets and divines to dream of it.

BEAUTIFUL FACE. (See Countenance.)

BEANS. To dream you are eating beans, always betokens trouble and dissensions. (See Vegetables.)

BEAR. To dream that you have seen a bear denotes you have a rich, puissant, inexpert, but cruel and audacious enemy.

BEARD. To dream you have one, is a sign of good fortune in love.

BED. (See Fire.)

BEES. To dream of bees is good and bad: good, if they sting not, but bad, if they sting the party dreaming, for then the bees do signify enemies; and therefore to dream that bees fly about your ears, shows your being beset with many enemies; but if you beat them off, without being stung by them, it is a sign of victory, and of your overcoming them. To dream of seeing bees, indicates profit to country people, and trouble to the rich; yet to dream that they make honey in any part of the house or tenement, is a sign of dignity, eloquence, and good success in business. To take bees, shows profit and gain, by reason of their honey and wax.

BEGGARS. To dream you see a beggar, foretells you will be surrounded with lovers. (See Alms.)

BEHEADING. To dream that one is beheaded, and that the head is separated from the body, denotes liberty to prisoners, health to the sick, comfort to those in distress; to creditors, payment of debts. To parents. good fortune, and that their cares and fears will be turned into joy and confidence in their children. If one dreams that a person of his acquaintance beheads him, he will share with him in his pleasures and honors. If any one dreams that a young child, who has not yet attained the age of his youth, hath cut off his head, if the dreamer be sick, he will not live long; if in health, he will get honor. (See Head.)

BIRDS. To dream you see many birds, denotes assemblies and suits at law. To dream of catching birds with nests, shows the entrapping or ensnaring of enemies by deceitful means. To dream of great birds is better for the rich than the poor. To dream of little birds the contrary. To dream that you hear little birds chirp is a good sign. To see birds fighting betokens adversity. To see birds fly over your head, shows prejudice by enemies. To see black-birds, denotes trouble. To hear birds sing, is joy and delight.

BIRDS'-NESTS. To dream you find one is a good sign. To dream you find one without either eggs or birds, shows you will meet with a great disappointment.

BIRDING. To dream you catch birds, is a sign of profit and pleasure.

BITE. To dream you are bitten signifies you will suffer the pangs of jealousy.

BLIND. To dream of being blind, shows a man shall be admonished to foresee his errors and avoid them, especially in love affairs. This dream also threatens the dreamer with

want of money—when a man at noonday cannot see a penny in his purse, which is a common kind of blindness.

BLOOD. To dream you vomit much blood, and of a good color, is good for him that is poor, for he shall get store of money. It is also very good for him who hath no children, and whose kindred are in a strange country: the first shall see a child of his own; the other his kindred returning home. To dream of carrying blood, is not good for them that desire to be hidden. To dream you vomit corrupt blood, is sickness to all. To cast a little blood in spitting, foretells sedition, as some have known by experience.

BLOWING THE FIRE. To dream of blowing the fire, denotes, to the rich, servitude; to the poor, profit. To dream of stirring up and blowing the fire, denotes also the stirring up of wrath, and that old quarrels, that have long lain dormant, shall be revived.

BLOWS. To dream you give blows is a sign of a law-suit. To dream you receive them—reconciliation with enemies.

BOAT. To dream you are in a boat upon a river, lake, or pond of clear water, is very good, and indicates joy, prosperity, and good success in affairs. If a man dream that he is walking in a boat, and recreating himself without fear, he will have comfort and success in his affairs; but if the water be rough and tempestuous, it falleth out contrary.

BOOKS. (See Reading.)

BOUQUET. To carry one, marriage; to destroy one, separation; to throw one away, displeasure. (See Flowers.)

BRASS. (See Metals.)

BREAD. To dream of eating such bread as is usual, or as the person dreaming is accustomed to, is good; but to dream of eating unusual bread is bad, and therefore for the poor to dream they eat white bread, denotes sickness; and for the rich to dream they eat brown bread, shows they shall meet with some obstructions in their affairs. To dream of rye bread is good for all, for it signifies health and content.

BREWING AND BAKING. To dream of brewing and baking, is a sign of an ill housewife, who lies dreaming in bed when she should be at work and doing her business.

BRIDGE. For one to dream that he goes over a broken bridge, betokens fear; and to dream you fall upon a bridge, is a sign of obstruction in business.

BROTH. To dream of eating broth, is a good sign, and indicates profit or gain.

BRETHREN. To dream that you discourse with your brethren, betokens vexations; because our brethren bring us nothing when they are born, but diminish our inheritance and succession, and are the cause that those things which would be all our own are divided into many parts between them and us. Timocrates dreamed that he buried, or caused to be interred, one of his brothers, departed, and a little while after, one of his chief adversaries died. To dream of the death of our brethren, signifieth, not only the loss of our enemies, but also deliverance or acquittance from some loss or hurt which attended us, and whereof we stood in fear; as it happened to Diocles, the grammarian, who sustained no loss of money, whereof he stood in doubt, and was afraid because he dreamed before that he saw his brother dead.

BULL. To dream you own a bull is a sign of gain. To dream you see a bull killed is a sign of affliction. To drive a bull signifies gayety. A black bull signifies deception and cheating; running, a secret divulged; at work, a fortune; drinking, a theft; without horns, peculation; fighting with another, fraternal affection. (See Cattle.)

BURIED ALIVE. For a man to dream he is buried alive, shows he is in danger of being unhappy and unfortunate during his life. To dream you see a burial is a sign of long life. (See Funeral and Grave.)

BUSINESS. To dream you manage business of great concernment shows you will meet obstructions.

BUTTERFLY. To dream of a butterfly is a sign you have an inconstant lover, or sweetheart.

CALF. To dream you see a calf is a sign of certain prosperity.

CAMEL. To dream of a camel is a sign of some great good fortune. A caravan of camels signifies a quickly dissipated fortune.

CANDLE. To dream one sees a candle extinguished, denotes sadness, sickness, and poverty. When one dreams he sees a shining lighted candle, it is a good sign to the sick, denoting recovery and health; and if he that dreams be unmarried, it shows he will speedily marry, have success, and prosper in his undertakings. To dream that you make candles, is a sign of rejoicing. To dream that you see candles not lighted, shows you shall have a reward for something you have done.

CAPON. To dream that a capon crows, indicates sadness and trouble.

CARAVAN. (See Camel.)

CARDS. Playing at cards, tables, or any other game in a dream, shows the party shall be very fortunate; and tables allude unto love, for love is the table, fancy the point that stands open; and he that dreams much of table playing shall be a great gamester, as well with Joan as my lady.

CARROTS. To dream of carrots denotes profit and strength to them who are at law for an inheritance; for we pluck them out of the ground with their heads, branches, strings and veins.

CART. To dream of being tied in a cart, to draw like a horse or an ox, denotes servitude and pain to everybody, how rich and mighty soever they be. To dream that you are carried in your cart or coach, to be drawn by men, signifies to have might and authority over many, and to have children of good behavior. As for travelers, it is to go slowly, but surely, when they have such a dream.

CAT. To dream of a cat signifies you will be robbed. To kill one, an averted danger; enraged, family quarrels.

CATTLE. To dream of keeping cattle, portends disgrace and loss to the rich, but profit to the poor. Also to dream of fat cattle shows a fruitful year; but lean cattle denotes scarcity. (See Cow and Bull.)

CHARIOT. To dream of guiding a chariot drawn by wolves, leopards, dogs, tigers, or such like beasts, is only good to those who have great enemies. To dream of being drawn in a chariot by men, is only good to those that desire to command and be obeyed; to others it denotes loss and discredit.

CHERRIES. To dream you eat ripe cherries denotes good luck, but sour cherries, signifies a lawsuit.

CHESS. To dream you are playing chess is a sign of discord with friends.

CHEESE. To dream you eat cheese is a sign of profit and gain.

CHESTNUTS. To dream of chestnuts portends home troubles.

CAULIFLOWER. (See Vegetables.)

CHILDREN. To dream that a man sees two or three children, shows he shall have cause of joy, and meet with good success in his business. When one dreams that he hath many small children, and that they seem to him to run about the house, and yet notwithstanding he hath none, it signifies it will be very difficult for him ever to have any, besides which, he that so dreams will have many cares and obstructions in his affairs. And here note that, among little children, it is better to dream that you see boys than girls. To dream of anything to befall little children, which is not proper to their age, is not good; as to dream that boys have beards and gray hairs, and that little girls should be married and have children, which betokens to them death.

CHURCH. To dream you are in church signifies prosperity in business. To see a church closed, great misfortune.

CLAMS. (Same as Oysters.)

CLOCK. To dream of a clock is a sure sign of happiness.

CLOAK. To dream that one has lost his cloak, is good if it be old, for thereby is signified that the party so dreaming shall have a new one; but if he dream of finding it again, then he shall have no change, but shall keep the old one still.

CLOTHES. (See Apparel.) If a man dream he has a new suit of clothes, it is a sign of honor. To dream that you see your clothes burned, denotes loss and damage. To dream that you see yourself in black clothes signifies joy. To dream that you take your clothes to put them on, denotes loss. If a man or woman dream they are meanly clothed, it betokens trouble and sadness. If one dream his clothes are dirty, or that he hath bad clothes tattered and much worn, it means shame. To dream your clothes are embroidered all over with gold, or any other kind of embroidery, signifies joy and honor.

CLOUDS. To dream of white clouds, is a sign of prosperity; clouds mounting high from the earth, denote voyages, and return of the absent, and revealing of secrets. Clouds red and inflamed, show an ill issue of affairs. To dream of smoky, dark, or obscure clouds, shows an ill time, or anger. (See Air.)

COACH. To dream of riding in a coach, shows that the party so dreaming shall love idleness, is given to pride, and shall die a beggar. To dream of coming out of a coach, denotes being degraded from great honor, and coming into disgrace upon a criminal account.

COAL-PITS. To dream of being at the bottom of coal-pits, indicates matching with a widow, for he that marries her must be a continual drudge, and yet shall never sound the depth of her policies.

COFFEE. To dream you are drinking coffee, is a sign that you have insincere friends who are plotting against you. To dream you see others drinking coffee signifies a domestic quarrel.

COLD. To suffer from cold is a sign of a joyous life. To have a cold signifies you have secret enemies.

CONCERT. To dream of a concert signifies a life of harmony with the one you love.

COOK. To dream you see a cook in the house, is good to those who would marry, for marriages are not good without a cook; it is also good for the poor, for they shall have goods, and ability to keep a good and long table; to the sick it is inflammation, heat and tears.

COPPER. (See Metals and Money.)

CORN. (See Vegetables.)

COUNTENANCE. To dream you see a comely countenance, unlike your own, betokens honor.

COW. To dream of a cow is a sign of prosperity and abundance. (See Cattle.)

CUCUMBERS. To dream of eating cucumbers denotes sickness and vain hopes, but to the sick it is a prognostic of recovery.

CUT. (See Fingers.)

DAGGER. To dream of a dagger, foretells that your dearest hope will be fulfilled.

DANCING. For a man to dream that he sees himself dance alone, or in the presence of his household, also to see his wife, children, or either of his parents dance, is good; for it shows abundance of mirth; but to him that is sick, or hath any disease about him, it is evil. (See Ball.)

DARK. To dream of being in the dark, and that he cannot find his way out of the room, or so that he loses his way in riding, or in going up a high pair of stairs, denotes that the party so dreaming shall be blinded with some passion, and much troubled.

DEAD MAN. To dream that you see a dead man, signifieth that he that dreams will be subject to the same passions and fortune as the party deceased had when alive, if he knew him.

DEAD. To dream of talking with dead folks, is a good auspicious dream; it shows great courage, and a very clear conscience. To dream a man is dead, who is alive and in health, denotes great trouble and being overthrown at law.

DEATH. To dream of death, signifies a wedding; for death and marriage represent one another. For the sick to dream they are married, or that they celebrate their weddings, is a sign of death, and signifies separation from her or his companions, friends, or parents; for the dead keep not company with the living. (See Marriage.)

DEBT. To dream of debt, we are to take notice, that the debtor and creditor represent life; wherefore, to the sick, the creditor urging and constraining is great danger, and receiving is death; for we owe a life to nature, our universal mother, which she makes us restore and pay.

DEVIL. To dream that one has seen the devil, and that he is tormented, or otherwise much terrified, is a sign the dreamer is in danger of being checked and punished by the law.

DICE. To dream of dice, is a sign of poverty and sickness.

DIGGING. To dream you are digging, is very good; but if you dream that your spades, or digging tools, seem to be lost, it portends loss of labor, dearth of corn, and ill-harvest weather.

DITCHES. To dream you see great ditches or precipices, and that you fall into them, is a sign that he who dreams will suffer much injury and hazard by his person, and his goods be in danger by fire. To dream you go over a ditch by a small plank, means much deceit by lawyers.

DOGS. When we dream of such dogs as belong to us, it signifies fidelity, courage and affection; but if we dream of those which belong to strangers, it means infamous enemies. To dream that a dog barks and tears our garments, betokens some enemy of mean condition slanders us, or endeavors to deprive us of our livelihood. To play with a dog, denotes you will suffer for former extravagance; to hunt with one, hope; one running, loss of a law-suit; to hear one howling, great danger; to lose one, want of success; one frisking about, loss of a friend; two fighting, a warning to beware of false friends.

DRAGON. To dream you see a dragon, is a sign you shall see some great magistrate; it implies also riches and treasure.

DRAWING. (See Pictures.)

DRESS. (See Apparel.)

DRINKING. To dream that you are drinking, when you are very dry, is an assured sign of sickness, especially if your dream be near the break of day, and the dreamer be of a sanguine complexion, and lying on the left side.

DROWNING. To dream you are drowning, is a sign you will make your fortune. To see another drowning, tells that your sorrow will have an end.

DUCK OR GOOSE. Profit and pleasure. To kill one, misfortune; to catch one, snare laid for the dreamer. (See Geese.)

EARTH. If a man dreams that he hath good lands, or earth well inclosed, bestowed upon him, with pleasant pastures, he will have a handsome wife. If you dream you see the earth black, that implies sorrow, melancholy, and the weakness of the brain.

ECLIPSE. For one to dream that he sees the sun in eclipse, means the loss of his father; but if he sees the moon eclipsed in his dream, it betokens the death of his mother; but if the party dreaming have neither father nor mother, then the death of the next nearest relation (See Sun and Moon.)

EGGS. To dream of eggs signifies that you will have success with all your undertakings. (See Hens.)

ELEPHANT. To dream that one sees an elephant, signifies the party shall be rich; for if one dreams he is carried on an elephant, he shall enjoy the estate of some great prince or lord; and if one dreams that he gives an elephant anything to eat or drink, it is a sign he shall wait upon some great lord to his advantage.

EVIL SPIRITS. Dreaming that evil spirits shall obstruct

thy doing good, under a show of devotion, shows thou wilt be obstructed in thy affairs by a hypocrite. And if thou dreamest that thou seest hideous physiognomies, things more than common shall be revealed to thee.

EYES. If any one dream he hath lost his eyes, it shows he will violate his word, or else that he or some of his children are in danger of death, or that he will never more see his friends again.

EYEBROWS. Dreaming the eyebrows are hairy, and of a good grace, is good, especially to women. But the eyebrows naked and without hair implies she will be afraid to marry. But if either man or woman dream their eyebrows are more comely and large than they used to be, it is a sign they will do feats in the matrimonial way.

EARTH-WORMS. Dreaming of earth-worms betokens secret enemies, that endeavor to ruin and destroy us.

FACE. To dream you see a fresh, taking, smiling face and countenance, is a sign of friendship and joy. Dreaming you see a meager, pale face, is a sign of trouble, poverty, and death. Dreaming one washes his face, implies repentance for sin; a black face is a sign of long life.

FALL. Dreaming you had a fall from a tree, been scratched by thorns, or otherwise prejudiced, signifies you shall lose your office, and be out of favor with grandees.

FARM. To dream of a farm signifies you will soon have anxious cares. (See Plowing.)

FARMER. (See Husbandry.)

FATHER-IN-LAW. To dream one sees his father-in-law, either dead or alive, is ill; especially if he dreams that he uses violence or threatening. And to dream that he uses gentle speech and good entertainment, implies vain hopes and deceit.

FAIRS. To dream of going to fairs, threatens the person so dreaming with having his pockets picked, which is usually done in those places.

FEAST. (See Banquet.)

FEET. To dream that a man's feet are cut off, betokens damage. Dreaming one hath a wooden leg, implies the alteration of your condition from good to bad, and from bad to worse.

FIELDS. Dreaming of fields and pleasant places shows a man that he will marry a discreet, chaste, and beautiful wife, and have handsome children. And to women it betokens a loving and prudent husband.

FIGS. Momentary pleasure. Dried, festivity; green, hope; to eat them, reverses.

FIGHTING. To dream of fighting, signifies opposition and

contention; and if the party dreams he is wounded in fighting, it implies loss of reputation and disgrace.

FINGERS. Dreaming you cut your fingers, or see them cut by another, betokens damage. To dream you lose some or all of your fingers, implies either the hurt or loss of servants. To scriveners, orators, and attorneys, it is a sign they shall want employment; to debtors, that they shall pay more than they owe; to usurers, loss by interest.

FIRE. When a man dreams of fire, or that he sees fire, it means the issue of his choler; and commonly they that dream of fire are active and furious; if a man dreams he is burnt by fire, a violent fever is prognosticated thereby. When a man dreams that his bed is on fire, and that he perished, it betokens damage, sickness, or death to his wife; and if the wife dream it, the same will happen to her husband. If one dream that the kitchen is on fire, that denotes death to his cook. (See Blazing Fire.)

FISH. If any one dreams he sees or catches large fish, it is a sign of profit. Dreaming you see fish of divers colors, means to the sick, poison; and to those in health, injuries, contention and grief.

FLAG. To dream of a flag signifies loss by fire.

FLATTERY. To dream one is pleasant and easily endures flattery, is not good; especially if one of our familiars, for it signifies to be betrayed by him.

FLEAS. To dream you see a flea, portends disappointment in some cherished design. To kill one, triumph over your enemies.

FLESH. If any one dreams he has increased in flesh, he will gain wealth. On the contrary, if you dream you have got thin, you will grow poor. If you dream your flesh is spotted or black, you will prove deceitful.

FLIES. Jealousy excited by the dreamer's success.

FLOWERS. If you dream of holding or smelling odoriferous flowers in their season, it means joy. On the contrary, to dream that you see or smell flowers out of season, if they be white, it denotes obstruction in business, and bad success; all other colors denote sickness. To gather flowers, lasting friendship; to cast away, despair, quarrels. (See Garden and Bouquet.)

FLUTE. To dream you hear a flute signifies your fondest hopes will be blighted. To dream you are playing the flute is a sign you will have a pleasant, prosperous life.

FRUIT. To dream you are eating good, sweet ripe fruit, denotes joy and happiness, but to dream you are eating sour and unripe fruit, signifies cares and contention.

FOX. A ruse to which the dreamer will fall victim. Killed, triumph over enemies; petted, abuse of confidence, unfortunate undertaking.

FUNERAL. To dream one goes to the funeral of a friend, is a good sign the dreamer shall have money, or marry a fortune. (See Buried Alive.)

GARDEN. To dream of walking in a garden, and gathering flowers, shows the person is given to pride and to have high thoughts of herself, but it also denotes a lasting friendship. If a man dream of seeing fair gardens, he will marry a chaste and beautiful wife. (See Flowers and Land.)

GEESE. If you dream of the cackling of geese, you will have an increase of business, and much profit. (See Duck.)

GIANT. If you dream of seeing a giant, or a large-sized man, it is a good sign.

GIBBET. To dream you see a person hanging on a gibbet, is a sign of damage and great affliction.

GIRDLE. Dreaming you are girt with a girdle, means labor and pains. If you dream you have a new girdle, it means honor.

GLASS. If one dreams that he hath had a glass given him full of water, he shall be married speedily, and his wife shall have children. But if the glass is cracked, he must look for sickness and loss.

GOAT. To dream of white goats is a sign of wealth and plenty, but black signify sickness and uncertain lawsuits.

GOLD. (See Metals and Money.)

GRAIN. If you dream of seeing and gathering grain, it denotes prosperity. If you dream of eating it in soup, it is bad.

GRAPES. Rejoicings, enjoyment. To eat them, joy, gain; to gather them, considerable increase of fortune; to throw them away, loss, care, and bitterness; to trample them under foot, abundance.

GRASSHOPPER. To dream of grasshoppers, portends a poor harvest.

GRAVE. If you dream of being put into a grave and buried, it presageth you shall die in a mean condition. (See Buried Alive.)

GROVES. Dreaming you have land and groves adjoining, denotes you will be married well, and be blessed with children.

GROUND. Dreaming you fall upon the ground, denotes dishonor, shame, and scandal.

GRANDFATHER. (See Predecessors.)

HAIR. For a man to dream his hair is long, like a woman's, denotes cowardice and effeminacy, and that the person dreaming will be deceived by a woman. If you dream you see a woman without hair, famine and sickness will ensue. If you see a man bald, and without hair, it signifies the contrary. If you dream you cannot pass the comb through your hair, and cannot disentangle it, it portends great trouble and lawsuits.

HATRED. Dreaming of hatred, or being hated, whether of friends or enemies, is an ill omen.

HEAD. To dream you have a great head, or a head bigger than ordinary, and very highly raised, denotes dignity. If you dream of your head being cut off by robbers and murderers, that indicates loss of children, relations, estate, or wife; and to a wife so dreaming, the loss of her husband. (See beheading.)

HEAVEN. Dreaming of heaven, and that you ascend up thither, is an indication of grandeur and glory.

HENS. If you dream you hear hens cackle, or that you catch them, it denotes joy, and an increase of property, and success in business. Dreaming you see a hen with her chickens, means loss and damage. If you see a hen lay eggs, it denotes gain. (See Chicken.)

HERBS. (See Vegetables.)

HILLS. To dream you are traveling over hills and wading through great difficulties, and meet with assistance in the way, shows that you shall have good counsel, and overcome all your troubles.

HORNS. If you dream of having horns on your head, it denotes grandeur. If you see a man with horns on his head, he is in danger of loss of his person and estate.

HORSES. If you dream of a horse, it is good sign; or if one dreams he mounts a horse, it is a happy omen. To dream you are riding on a tired horse, shows one shall be desperately in love; to kill one, disunion, grief; to dream of a black horse, denotes partial success; a white one, unexpected good fortune; to see one wounded, failure in undertakings; to shoe one, good luck; to dream you see a dead horse tells of misfortune. (See Plowing and Saddle.)

HOUSE. To dream one builds a house, denotes comfort. Dreaming of building houses, wearing fine clothes, and talking with ladies, is a sign that the parties will suddenly marry.

HUSBANDRY. If you dream of a plow, it is good for marriages. To dream of the yoke, is good, but not for servants. (See Plowing and Manure.)

ICE. Denotes a good harvest to husbandmen; and to merchants, and to other men of employment, it betokens hindrance in their negotiations and voyages.

IMAGES. Dreaming you make images of men, denotes you will shortly be married and have many children, and very like yourselves.

IRON. (See Metals.)

JOLLITY. Dreaming of jollity, feasts, and merry-makings, is a good and prosperous dream, and promiseth great preferment.

KEYS. To dream you lose your keys, denotes anger. But to dream you have a bunch of keys, and that you give them to those that desire them of you, shows goodness to the poor. A key seen in a dream, to him that would marry, denotes he shall have a handsome wife and a maid.

KING. Dreaming you discourse with a king, implies honor.

KNEES. Dreaming your knees are strong and sturdy, shows health and strength to go through your various avocations; but to dream they are weak, the contrary. If a man dreams that by the strength of his knees he can run swiftly, he shall be happy in all his undertakings. If it be a woman, she will be ready and willing to obey her husband, and be careful to govern her family.

KNIFE. To dream you bestow a knife upon any one denotes injustice and contention.

LAND. If a man dreams he has good lands, well inclosed, he shall have a handsome wife. If he dreams that the lands have gardens, fountains, pleasant groves, and orchards, he will marry a discreet, chaste, and beautiful wife, and have children.

LAMBS. To dream of lambs in the fields signifies peace, tranquillity; to keep them, profit; to carry one, success; to buy one, great surprise; to kill one, secret grief: to find one, a gain of a lawsuit: to eat, tears.

LARKS. Riches.   Roasted, accidents in the dreamer's house.

LAUREL. If you dream you see a laurel-tree, it denotes victory and pleasure; and if you be married, it betokens inheritance of possessions. Dreaming you see or smell laurel, if it be a married woman, she shall have children; if a maid, she will be suddenly married.

LEAD. (See Metals.)

LEG. (See Feet and Knees.)

LEMONS. To dream of lemons denotes the dreamer will have good luck.

LEEKS. (See Vegetables.)

LETTERS. Dreaming you learn letters, is good to the ignorant; but to one that has learned his letters it is not good.

LETTUCE. (See Vegetables.)

MAD. For a man to dream he is mad, and is guilty of extravagancies, he shall be long-lived, and become of great consequence.

MALLOWS. If you dream of eating mallows, it denotes exemption from trouble, and dispatch of business.

MANURE. Dreaming that you manure or cultivate the earth, is a sign of melancholy to those who are in good condition, but to laborers it signifies gain and a plentiful crop.

MARJORAM. Dreaming that you smell marjoram, denotes trouble, labor, and sadness.

MARRIAGE. To dream that you do the act of marriage, denotes danger. Marriage, or the wedding of a woman, is a token of the death of some friend; and for a man to dream that he is newly married, and that he hath had to do with his new wife, it denotes some evil accident will befall him. (See Death.)

MARSHES. Dreaming of marshes is good only for farmers; to all others they are a sign of hindrances of business.

MARTYR. If one dreams that he dies for religion, the person will arrive at a great point of honor; and it denotes that his soul will be happy hereafter.

MEASLES. If any one dreams he hath the measles, it denotes he shall gain wealth, but it shall be with infamy.

MELONS. Dreaming of melons, is to sick persons a prognostic of recovery, by reason of their juicy substance.

METALS. To dream of metals has different significations and interpretations according to the metal you dream of. To enable our readers to more readily discover the meaning of ther dreams, we subjoin a list of the metals with their explanations. *Brass.* To dream you see a brass ornament, is a sign your sweetheart will be false to you. To see any one working in brass, or cleaning that metal, is a sign you will hear of the death of a distant relative who will leave you a legacy. *Copper.* To dream of copper, signifies that your sweetheart is deceitful and loves another, it also shows secret enemies. *Gold.* To dream of receiving gold is a good sign, and shows you will be successful in all your undertakings. To dream you pay gold betokens increase of friends. *Iron.* For one to dream that he is hurt with iron, signifies that he shall receive some damage. *Lead.* To dream of lead denotes sickness, but to dream of leaden bullets, good news. If you dream you are wounded by a leaden bullet it is a sign you will be successful in love. *Quicksilver.* To dream of this metal is a sign your friends will all be false to you, it is also a sign of losses in property. *Silver.* To dream that you are presented with spoons, or any silver plate for household use, foretells that you, or some near relative, will shortly marry, but not happily; if you dream of buying these articles, it is a sign of poverty; to dream of silver dollars, or bars of silver used in commerce, is a sign that you will lose money by speculation.

Steel. To break a piece in a dream, shows that you will over-come your enemies; if you only touch it, your position in life is secure; if you try to bend it, and cannot, you will meet with many serious accidents.

MICE. To dream of mice foretells business affairs embarrass-ed through the machinations of dangerous friends.

MILK. To dream you drink milk, is an extraordinary good sign; and to dream you see breasts full of milk, denotes gain.

MOLE. Dreaming of a mole, denotes a man blind by incon-venience and labor in vain, and also that he who would be secret shall be disclosed by himself.

MONKEYS. Dreaming of monkeys, shows you have mali-cious, strange, and secret enemies.

MOON. If any one dream that he sees the moon shine, it shows that his wife loves him extremely well; it also implies the getting of silver; for, as the sun represents gold, so the moon doth silver. Dreaming you see the moon darkened, denotes the death or sickness of your wife, mother, sister, or daughter; loss of money, or danger in a voyage or journey, especially if it be by water; or else it denotes a distemper in the brain or eyes. To dream you see the moon darkened, and grow clear and bright again, implies gain to the woman that dreams, and to the man joy and prosperity; but to dream that you see the moon clear, and afterwards cloudy, presageth the contrary. To dream you see the moon in the form of a full white face, implies to the virgin speedy marriage; to the married woman, that she will have a handsome daughter. If the husband dream it, it implies that his wife will have a son. To dream you see the moon at full, is a good sign to hand-some women, of their being beloved by those who view them; but it is bad for such as conceal themselves, as thieves and murderers, for they will certainly be discovered; but it signi-fies death to those that are sick, and to seafaring men. To dream the moon shines about your bed, implies grace, par-don, and deliverance by some woman. To dream you see the new moon, is a sign of expedition in business. Dreaming you see the moon decrease, betokens the death of some great per-son. To dream you see the moon pale is joyfulness. To dream you see the moon dyed with blood, indicates travel or pilgri-mage. Dreaming you see the moon fall from the firmament, is a sign of sickness. To dream you see two moons appear, betokens increase of sorrow. Eclipse of the moon signifies gain in business. (See Eclipse.)

MONEY. To dream of losing money denotes losses in busi-ness. To find money, if gold, or large bank bills, is a good omen, and signifies success in all your undertakings; but to dream you find small silver or copper coin foretells a discovery made too late to be of any benefit to you. To dream you are melting or see money melted or bank bills burned, presages disappointment in some cherished design. To dream you throw money away foretells chagrin and want. To dream you change money foretells inconstancy in a lover or sweetheart. To dream you have money given or paid to you, implies success in love affairs, and much domestic happiness. To dream of counterfeit money is a bad omen, and foretells quarrels, sickness, and secret enemies; it also presages domestic unhappiness. To dream of money in bags or boxes, also denotes misfortune of some kind. Thus Shylock, in the "Merchant of Venice," says:

> "There is some ill a brewing towards my rest,
> For I did dream of money-bags to-night."

MOTHER-IN-LAW. Dreaming you see a mother-in-law, dead or alive, is ill; especially if you dream she uses violence or threatening. To dream she uses gentle speech, and gives good entertainment, implies vain hope and deceit.

MOUTH. The mouth is the door of all the internal parts of the body, within which they are all inclosed. If, therefore, one dreams that his mouth is wider than ordinary, his family will be enriched, and he will become more opulent than formerly. If any one dreams that the breath which comes out of his mouth is offensive, it implies he shall be despised by all people, and hated by his servants.

MULBERRY-TREE. If one dreams he sees a mulberry-tree, it implies an increase, with abundance of goods and children.

MUSIC. (See Plays). To dream you hear melodious music, which is even ready to ravish your ears, implies the parties dreaming shall hear some very acceptable news, with which they shall be greatly delighted. But if they dream that they hear harsh and ill-tuned music, it means the contrary, and that they shall soon meet with such tidings as they do not wish to hear.

NAILS. Dreaming that one's nails are longer than usual, is a sign of profit; and the contrary, loss and discontent. To dream that one's nails are cut off, shows to the party so dreaming that he shall suffer loss and disgrace, and have contention with his friends and relations.

NAVIGATION. To dream of being in a ship or boat, in danger of oversetting and shipwreck, is a sign of danger, unless the party be a prisoner or captive; and in that case it denotes liberty and freedom. He that dreams he falls into the water or sea, and that he awakes starting, it signifies that he will spend his days and means in profligacy. (See Shipwreck.)

NETTLES. Dreaming of nettles, and that you sting yourself with them, shows that you will venture hard for what you desire to obtain; and if they are young folks that dream thus, it shows they are in love, and are willing to take a nettle though they are stung thereby.

NIGHTMARE. To dream of being ridden by the nightmare. is a sign that a woman so dreaming shall be suddenly after married, and that a man shall be ridden and domineered over by a fool.

NIGHT-WALKING. To dream of walking in the night, implies trouble and melancholy.

NOSE. Dreaming one has a fair and great nose, is good to all; for it implies subtlety of sense, providence in affairs, and acquaintance with great persons. But to dream one has no nose, means the contrary; and to a sick man, death; for dead men's heads have no nose. If any one dreams his nose is larger than ordinary, he will become rich and powerful, provident and subtle, and be well received among grandees. Dreaming one has two noses, implies discord and quarrels. If one dreams that his nose is grown so big that it is deformed and hideous to the sight, he will live in prosperity and abundance, but never gain the love of the people. If any one dreams his nose is stopped, so that he hath lost his scent, it signifies he is in danger from a supposed friend.

OAK. To dream one sees a stately oak, is a sign of long life, riches, and gain to the dreamer. (See Plant.)

OIL. Dreaming you are anointed with oil, is good for women; but for men it is ill, and implies shame.

OLD WOMEN. To dream that you are courted by an old woman, and that you marry her, shows you shall have good luck in prosecuting your affairs, but not without some reproaches from the world.

OLIVE TREES. To dream you see an olive tree with olives, denotes peace, delight, concord, liberty, dignity, and fruition of your desires. In dreams, the olive tree means the wife, and therefore it is good to dream that it is flourishing well, bearing fair and ripe fruit in season. To dream you beat the olives down, is good for all but servants.

ONIONS. (See Vegetables.)

ORANGES. Dreaming that one sees and eats oranges, implies wounds, grief, and vexation, whether they be ripe or not.

ORCHARD. (See Land, Fruit, Pears, Apples and Trees.)

ORGANS. To dream that you hear the sound of organs, betokens joy.

OWLS. To dream of owls, old barns, church-yards, &c., betokens much melancholy, as also imprisonment, keeping one's chamber, and sickness; and it denotes the same also to dream of an owlet or bat.

OYSTERS. To dream of opening and eating oysters, shows great hunger, which the party dreaming should suddenly sustain; or else that he should take great pains for his living, as they do that open oysters.

PAPER. To dream you write on or read in paper denotes news. To dream you blot or tear your paper indicates the well ordering of business.

PATHS. Dreaming one walks in large, plain, and easy paths betokens health to the dreamer; and paths which are narrow, crooked, and rough signify the contrary.

PEACHES. To dream you gather peaches is a sign of good fortune and prosperous undertakings. To dream you eat ripe peaches is a sign you will have great domestic happiness, but to eat unripe peaches denotes a quarrel.

PEARS. (Same as Peaches.)

PEACOCK. To dream you see a peacock is a sign you will marry a handsome wife, and that you will grow rich, and be in great honor. And if a woman has such a dream, it shows her husband shall be a pretty man, but a sot.

PEAS. Dreaming of peas well boiled denotes good success and expedition. (See Vegetables.)

PICTURES. To dream one draws pictures betokens joy without profit.

PIGS. To dream of a pig denotes assured gain. To dream of a dead pig is a sign that you will get a letter containing good news.

PIGEONS. To dream you see pigeons is a good sign; to wit, that you will have content and delight at home, and success in affairs abroad. To dream that you see a white pigeon flying denotes consolation, devotion, and success in good undertakings. Wild pigeons signify wild and dissolute women, and tame pigeons signify virtuous women.

PIT. Dreaming you see a pit full of fair water in a field, where there is none at all, is a good dream; for he who dreams this is a thriving man and will suddenly be married, if he be not so already, and will have good and obedient children. To dream you see a pit whose water overflows the banks, implies loss of substance, or the death of wife and children; and if the wife have the same dream, it shows her death or the loss of her substance. To dream you see a friend fall into a pit, shows that such a person is then near his end; and if it be a parent, aunt or child, that you dream falls, expect to see the death of such a relation very suddenly.

PLANT. To dream that any plant cometh out of one's body, is death. To dream of plants quick in growth, as the vine and the peach tree, implies that the good or evil portended us shall quickly happen; but to dream of trees and plants that are slow in growing, as the oak, olive, cypress, &c., shows that the good or evil that shall happen to us shall be long in coming. (See Trees.)

PLAYS. Dreaming you see a comedy, farce, or some other recreation, indicates good success in business. To dream you see a tragedy acted, implies labor, loss of estate, with grief and affliction. To dream one plays, or sees another play upon a flute, violin, or other musical instrument, betokens good news, concord, and a good correspondence between man and wife, master and servant, prince and subject. To dream one plays tunes on small bells denotes discord and disunion between subjects and servants. To dream you play, or hear playing on wind instruments, as flutes, flageolets or small bagpipes, or other such instruments, shows trouble, contention, and being overthrown at law. If any one dreams he plays at any of those plays which company use to divert themselves — as, at questions and commands, cross-purposes, blind-man's buff, hot cockles, barley-break, and such like—it implies prosperity, joy, pleasure, health, and concord among friends and relations.

PLOWING. Dreaming of plowing is good, but if the horses seem to sink into the ground, it portends loss of labor, dearth of corn, and ill-harvest weather; but to plow on a hill, and on a sudden to be loosening the team, and setting them up in a stable, doth show a lazy disposition in the plowman, and also that the horses shall not stand, but fall sick in the stable. (See Farm, Manure and Husbandry.)

PLUMS. To dream a friend gives you a sour plum, is a sign he will quarrel with you, but if he presents you with a ripe plum, it denotes he will do you a great service.

POCKET-BOOK. (See Purse.)

POMEGRANATE. If a man dream that he hath gathered the fruit of a pomegranate tree, he will be enriched by some wealthy person; but if the pomegranate be not ripe, it denotes sickness and affliction by some person wickedly disposed.

POT-HERBS. To dream of pot-herbs, especially such as have a strong smell, portends a discovery of hidden secrets and domestic jars.

PRAYERS. Dreaming you put up prayers or supplications to God, implies happiness. The prayers of beggars, and of the poor and miserable, signify care and anger to those who dream thereof; for no one requesteth of another without affliction; and none that are afflicted have reason and consideration, by reason whereof they are importunate, and cause trouble and hindrance.

PREDECESSORS. To dream of predecessors, as grandfathers, and other ancestors, implies care. (See Relations Deceased.)

PURSE. To dream that one hath lost his purse or pocket-book, is good and auspicious, if it be old and empty; for then thereby it is a sign that the party dreaming shall either have a new one, or one that is full; but if he dreamed he found it again, he must even be content with the old, for he is like to have no other. To dream you find a purse or pocket-book full of money, is a sign of good luck. (See Money.)

QUAGMIRE. Dreaming one has fallen into a quagmire, shows the party so dreaming shall meet with such obstructions in his affairs, as shall be very difficult to overcome.

QUARRELS. If a man dream of quarrels and fighting, he shall hear some unlooked-for news of women, or embrace some joy he thought not of.

QUICKSILVER. (See Metals.)

QUINCE. To dream one sees quinces, shows that they shall meet with some changes in their affairs, which shall be for the better.

RABBIT. Black, trouble; white friendship; a warren, expensive pleasures.

RADISHES. To dream that one eats or smells of radishes, signifies a discovery of hidden secrets and domestic jars.

RAIN. To dream of a gentle rain is a good omen, as it foretells success in any undertaking; if you dream of a violent rain-storm, accompanied by wind, and thunder and lightning, it predicts much trouble and misfortune, though ultimate success in your undertakings. (See Shower and Tempest.)

RAINBOW. It is an excellent dream to imagine you see a brilliant rainbow—the brighter the better; it denotes health and general prosperity; to lovers it foretells a happy marriage, and riches. A young girl who dreams of a rainbow will either get an agreeable lover or a present.

RASPBERRIES. Rejoicings, gain, profit. To eat them, a sign that the dreamer will be deceived by a woman; to throw them away, troubles caused by the envy of others.

RATS. Secret enemies, treason; white, triumph of the dreamer over them.

READING. To dream you are reading romances, comedies or other diverting books, signifies joy and comfort. To dream you read serious books, and of some divine science, denotes wisdom.

RELATIONS DECEASED. To dream one sees and discourses with father, mother, wife, brother, sister, or some other of his relations and friends, though they are dead, is an advertisement for the party to mind his affairs, and to behave him-self properly in the world. (See Predecessors.)

REPTILE. (See Alligator and Serpents.)

RICE. To dream of eating rice, denotes abundance of obstruction.

RIDE. To dream you ride with a company of men, is very lucky and profitable; but with women, it signifies misfortune and deceit. (See Saddle.)

RINGS. To dream of rings, betokeneth weddings, because they are then required.

RIVER. To dream you see a river, water clear and calm, presages good to all persons. To dream of swimming in a great river, signifies future peril and danger. (See Boat.)

ROOTS. All roots which have a strong smell in eating, sig-nify the revealing of secrets and anger. Roots which are pared or scraped before they are eaten, signify hurt, by rea-son of the superfluity which is cast away.

ROSES. To dream of seeing and smelling roses in the sea-son of the year, is a good sign for all persons. If the dream be when roses are out of season, it signifies the contrary. Also to dream of gathering roses, denotes the want of frui-tion, and folly of love. But to dream you see red roses, is a sign of joy, recreation, pleasure and delight.

RUE. (See Vegetables.)

RYE BREAD. (See Bread.)

SADDLE. To dream you were riding a horse without a sad-dle, signifies poverty, disgrace, and shame to the dreamer.

SEA. To dream of walking upon the sea, is good to him who would travel, as also to a servant, and to him who would take a wife; for the one shall enjoy his wife, and the other shall have his master at his own pleasure.

SERPENTS. To dream you see a serpent turning and wind-ing himself, signifies danger and imprisonment; it denotes, also, sickness and hatred. To dream you see many serpents, signifies you will be deceived by your wife.

SHEEP. To dream of sheep foretells great gain.

SHIPWRECK. To dream you see a shipwreck, is most dan-gerous to all, except those who are detained by force; for to them it signifieth releasing and liberty. (See Navigation.)

SHOWER. If one dream he sees a soft shower, without storm, tempest, or wind, it signifies gain. (See Rain.)

SKY. (See Clouds, Rainbow, Stars, Sun, Moon, and Eclipse.)

SINGING. If any one dream he sings, it signifies he will be affected, and weep. To dream you hear singing, or playing in concert upon instruments, signifies consolation in ad-versity, and recovery of health to those that are sick.

SILVER. (See Metals and Money.)

SNAKE. (See Serpents.)

SOUP. (See Broth.)

SPIDER. At night, success, money; in the morning, a law-suit; to kill one, pleasure.

STAG. Gain. To kill one, scandal propagated in the neighborhood; to chase one, loss through a failure in business.

STARS. To dream you see the sky clear, and full of stars, denotes great happiness. (See Sun, Moon, Eclipse, Sky, and Clouds.)

STEEL. (See Metals.)

STRAWBERRIES. Unexpected good fortune.

SUN. Bright, discovery of secrets; clouded, bad news; rising, success; setting, losses; eclipse of the sun, a sudden loss. (See Eclipse.)

TAPESTRY. To dream that one makes tapestry, signifies joy. To dream you see tapestry, denotes treachery, deceit and cozenage.

TAVERN. To dream you are in a tavern, and feasting with your companions, signifies joy and comfort.

TEETH. To dream you lose a tooth, is a sign you will soon lose a friend.

TEMPESTS. To dream of great and long-continuing tempests, signifies affliction, troubles, dangers, losses, and peril; to the poorer sort they denote repose. (See Rain.)

THORNS. Pain, disappointment. To be pricked by them, loss of money.

TIN. (See Metals.)

TORTOISE OR TURTLE. Delays and vexations in business. To eat, adjustment of affairs.

TREASURE. To dream you find treasure hidden in the earth, is evil, whether it be little or great; for they open the earth for the dead as well as for treasure.

TREES. Green, hope; shattered by a storm, domestic quarrels; withered, grief; leafless, deceit; in bud, success; cut down, a robbery; to climb one, change of employment. (See Plants, Orchard and Fall.)

TURNIPS. (See Vegetables.)

VINEGAR. To dream that you drink vinegar, betokens sickness.

VIRGIN. To dream you discourse with the Virgin Mary signifies joy and consolation; but a virgin dreaming she has lost her virtue, denotes she will give herself up to the first she likes.

VOMIT. To dream of vomiting, whether of blood, meat or phlegm, signifies to the poor, profit; to the rich, hurt; for the first can lose nothing till they have it, but the others, who have goods already, shall come to lose them. (See Blood.)

VEGETABLES. Wearisome toil; to gather them, quarrels; to eat them, losses in business. *Cabbage.* Health, long life. *Cauliflower.* Sickness, infidelity. *Beans.* Criticism; green, considerable loss. *Peas.* Good fortune. *Asparagus.* Profit, success. *Artichokes.* Pain, embarrassment. *Turnips.* Annoyance, disappointment. *Cucumber.* Serious indisposition. *Onions.* Dispute with inferiors. *Leeks.* Labor. *Lettuce.* Poverty. *Garlic.* A woman's deception. *Rue.* Family annoyances. *Herbs.* Prosperity; to eat, grief. *Corn.* Riches and happiness.

WALNUTS. To dream that one sees and eats walnuts, or hazel-nuts, signifies difficulty and trouble.

WASPS. To dream of wasps, is a sign you will be annoyed by enemies.

WATCH. To dream that in the night one sitteth up, and watcheth in the chamber, signifies, to the rich, great affairs; to the poor, and those that would use any subtleties or deceits, it is good; for the first shall not be without work and gain, and the others, undergoing their first attempts with great subtlety, shall come to the height of their enterprise.

WATER. (See Boats, Bath, Drinking, Glass, Navigation, Rivers and Showers.) To drink it, false security; to fall into, reconciliation; to bathe in running, disappointment; in stagnant, misfortune.

WEDDINGS. (See Marriage and Death.) For a man that is sick, to dream that he is wedded to a maid, shows he shall die quickly. If one dreams he is wedded to a deformed woman, it signifies discontent; if to a handsome woman, it denotes joy and profit.

WIFE. If a man dreams he sees his wife married to another, it betokens a change of affairs, or else of separation. If a man's wife dream she is married to any other than her own husband, she shall be separated from him, or see him dead.

WINE. Signifies prosperity; white, the friendship of great personages; red, joy, happiness; upset, a disaster in the family.

WRITING. (See Paper.)

WOLF. Enmity. To kill one, gain, success; to pursue one, dangers averted or overcome.

WORMS. (See Earth Worms.)

ZINC. (See Metals.)

MOLES.

THEIR SIGNIFICATIONS, EITHER IN MEN OR WOMEN.

These significant marks of the body are very remarkable guides either to the good or bad fortunes of any one.

A mole on the left side of a man, denotes danger and strangling; in a woman, sorrow, and great pain in child-birth.

A mole on the left cheek, foretells fruitfulness in either sex, as does one on the nose.

A mole on the upper lip, shows happiness in marriage.

A mole on the breast, shows affection, loyalty, strength, and courage, which will gain honor.

A mole on the naval, shows many children to a woman; and in man, that he shall be vigorous.

A mole in the midst of the forehead, shows wisdom and conduct in the management of affairs. ⚬

A mole on the right cheek, shows the party too much beloved, and will come unto great fortune.

A mole on the left shoulder, shows sorrow and labor.

A mole on the throat, denotes the party a great glutton, and by excess will undergo a great disease, and, peradventure, sudden death.

A mole on the right eye, shows loss of sight.

A mole on the forehead of a man or woman, denotes they shall grow rich, being beloved of their friends and neighbors.

A mole on the eyebrows, the men incontinent, and given to women; but if a woman, it shows she will have a good husband.

A mole on the nose, shows that the party loves pleasure more than anything else.

A mole on the neck, shows a man to be prudent in his actions; but a woman of a weak judgment, apt to believe the worst of her husband.

CHARMS AND CEREMONIES.

THE CHARMS OF ST. CATHERINE.

This day falls on the 25th of November, and must be thus celebrated. Let any number of young women, not exceeding seven or less than three, assemble in a room, where they are sure to be safe from interlopers; just as the clock strikes eleven at night, take from your bosom a sprig of myrtle, which you must have worn there all day, and fold it up in a bit of tissue paper, then light up a small chafing dish of charcoal, and on it let each maiden throw nine hairs from her head, and a paring of her toe and finger nails, then let each sprinkle a small quantity of myrtle and frankincense in the charcoal, and while the odoriferous vapor rises, fumigate your myrtle (this plant or tree is consecrated to Venus) with it.   Go to bed while the clock is striking twelve, and you will be sure to dream of your future husband, and place the myrtle exactly under your head.   Observe, it is no manner of use trying this charm, if you are not a real virgin, and the myrtle hour of performance must be passed in strict silence.

HOW TO MAKE YOUR LOVER OR SWEETHEART COME.

If a maid wishes to see her lover, let her take the following method.   Prick the third or wedding finger of your left hand with a sharp needle (beware a pin), and with the blood write your own and lover's name on a piece of clean writing paper, in as small a compass as you can, and encircle it with three round rings of the same crimson stream, fold it up, and exactly at the ninth hour of the evening, bury it with your own hand in the earth, and tell no one.   Your lover will hasten to you as soon as possible, and he will not be able to rest until he sees you, and if you have quarreled, to make it up.   A young man may also try this charm, only instead of the wedding finger, let him pierce his left thumb.

APPLE PARINGS.

On the 28th of October, which is a double Saint's day, take an apple, pare it whole, and take the paring in your right hand, and standing in the middle of the room, say the following verse:

St. Simon and Jude
On you I intrude,
By this paring I hold to discover,
Without any delay,
To tell me this day,
The first letter of my own true lover.

Turn round three times, and cast the paring over your left shoulder, and it will form the first letter of your future husband's surname; but if the paring breaks into many pieces, so that no letter is discernible, you will never marry; take the pips of the same apple, put them in spring water, and drink them.

TO KNOW HOW SOON A PERSON WILL BE MARRIED.

Get a green pea-pod, in which are exactly nine peas, hang it over the door, and then take notice of the next person who comes in, who is not of the family, and if it proves a bachelor, you will certainly be married within that year.

On any Friday throughout the year—Take rosemary flowers, bay leaves, thyme, and sweet marjoram, of each a handful; dry these, and make them into a fine powder; then take a teaspoonful of each sort, mix the powders together; then take twice the quantity of barley flour and make the whole into cake with the milk of a red cow. This cake is not to be baked, but wrapped in clean writing paper, and laid under your head any Friday night. If the person dreams of music, she will wed those she desires, and that shortly; if of fire, she will be crossed in love; if of a church, she will die single. If anything is written or the least spot of ink is on the paper, it will not do.

TO KNOW WHAT FORTUNE YOUR FUTURE HUSBAND WILL BE.

Take a walnut, a hazel-nut, and nutmeg; grate them together, and mix them with butter and sugar, and make them up into small pills, of which exactly nine must be taken on going to bed; and according to her dreams, so will be the state of the person she will marry. If a gentleman, of riches; if a clergyman, of white linen; if a lawyer, of darkness; if a tradesman, of odd noises and tumults; if a soldier or sailor, of thunder and lightning; if a servant, of rain.

TO KNOW IF A WOMAN WITH CHILD WILL HAVE A GIRL OR BOY.

Write the proper names of the father and the mother, and of the month she conceived with child, and likewise adding all the numbers of those letters together, divide them by seven; and then if the remainder be even, it will be a girl; if uneven, it will be a boy.

TO KNOW IF A CHILD NEW-BORN SHALL LIVE OR NOT.

Write the proper names of the father and mother, and of the day the child was born, and put to each letter its number, as you did before, and unto the total sum, being collected together, put twenty-five, and then divide the whole by seven; and then, if it be even, the child shall die; but if it be uneven, the child shall live.

TO KNOW IF ANY ONE SHALL ENJOY THEIR LOVE OR NOT.

Take the number of the first letter of your name, the number of the planet, and the day of the week; put all these together, and divide them by thirty; if it be above, it will come to your mind, and if below to the contrary; and mind that number which exceeds not thirty.

MIDSUMMER-DAY CHARM, TO KNOW YOUR HUSBAND'S TRADE.

Exactly at twelve, on Midsummer-day, place a bowl of water in the sun, pour in some boiling pewter as the clock is striking, saying thus:

> Here I try a potent spell,
> Queen of love, and Juno tell,
> In kind union unto me,
> What my husband is to be,
> This the day, and this the hour,
> When it seems you have the power
> For to be a maiden's friend,
> So, good ladies, condescend.

A tobacco-pipe full is enough. When the pewter is cold, take it out of the water, and drain it dry in a cloth, and you will find the emblems of your future husband's trade quite plain. If more than one, you will marry twice; if confused and no emblems, you will never marry; a coach shows a gentleman for you.

A CHARM FOR DREAMING.

When you go to bed, place under your pillow a Common Prayer Book, open at the part of the Matrimonial service, in which is printed, "With this ring I thee wed," etc., place on it a key, a ring, a flower and a sprig of willow, a small heart cake, a crust of bread, and the following cards, the ten of clubs, nine of hearts, ace of spades, and the ace of diamonds; wrap all these round in a handkerchief of thin gauze or muslin; on getting into bed cross your hands and say:

> Luna ever woman's friend,
> To me they goodness condescend;
> Let me this night in visions see,
> Emblems of my destiny.

If you dream of storms, trouble will betide you; if the storm ends in a fine calm, so will your fate; if of a ring, or of the ace of diamonds, marriage; bread, an industrious life; cake, a prosperous life; flowers, joy; willow, treachery in love; spades, death; diamonds, money; clubs, a foreign land; hearts, illegitimate children; keys, that you will rise to great trust and power, and never know want; birds, that you will have many children; geese, that you will marry more than once.

THE FLOWER AUGURY.

If a young man or woman receives a present of flowers, or a nosegay from their sweetheart, unsolicited, for if asked for, it destroys the influence of the spell; let them keep them in the usual manner in cold water four-and-twenty hours, then shift the water, and let them stand another twenty four hours, then take them, and immerse the stalks in water nearly boiling, leave them to perish for three hours, then look at them; if they are perished, or drooping, your lover is false; if revived and blooming, you will be happy in your choice.

HOW TO TELL BY A SCREW, WHETHER YOUR SWEETHEART LOVES YOU OR NOT.

Get a small screw, such as the carpenters use for hanging closet-doors, and after making a hole in a plank with a gimlet of a proper size, put the screw in, being careful to oil the end with a little sweet oil. After having done this, take a screw-driver and drive the screw home, but you must be sure and observe how many turns it takes to get the screw in so far that it will go no farther. If it requires an *odd* number of turns you can rest assured that your sweetheart does not love you yet, and perhaps is enamored of some other person; but if the number of turns is an *even* number, be happy, for your sweetheart adores you, and lives only in the sunshine of your presence.

EVENTS FORETOLD BY PLANETS.

JANUARY.—*Aquarius, or the Water-bearer*

ABOUT the twentieth of the month the sun enters this sign: a man born at this period will be of an unruly, restless, fickle, and boisterous disposition; will be given to all whims and strange fancies; will undertake anything, however difficult, to accomplish any object he may have in view; not contented long in one place; soon affronted—slow to forgive; suspicious and always imagining danger, and, instead of endeavoring to subdue trouble, meeting it half way. In life he will be moderately successful, and enjoy a portion of happiness. In love he will display an amorous disposition, and be passionately attached to his mistress, until she yields to his wishes, or marries him; he will then grow indifferent, and rove until some other object fixes his attention.

A woman born at this time will be of a studious, industrious, and sedentary disposition—will be much attached to the employment she is brought up to; in love she will be constant and moderate—she will make a kind and tender mother, and an affectionate wife.

FEBRUARY.—*Pisces, or the Fishes.*

About the twentieth of the month the sun enters this sign; a man born at this time will be designing, intriguing, selfish, unfaithful to his engagement; he will be mean and subservient to those whom he thinks he can make useful to his schemes; but his end once obtained, he will take every opportunity to injure and betray them; in poverty he will be a sycophant, in prosperity a tyrant—haughty to equals and inferiors. In life he will generally be unsuccessful, although for a time he will often appear to have succeeded; in love he will, be careless, indifferent, and unsteady—he will make a severe father and an unkind husband.

A woman born at the same period will be of obliging manners, delicate in her ideas, open and sincere in her friendships, an enemy to deceit—in love she will be faithful, and moderately inclined to the joys of Venus; she will be affectionate to her family; make a good and tender mother, and be a prosperous and excellent wife.

MARCH.—*Aries, or the Ram.*

About the twentieth of the month the sun enters this sign: a man born at this period will be of a bashful, meek, and irresolute disposition, hard to provoke to a quarrel, but difficult to be appeased when roused; in life he will be for the most part happy and contented—in love he will be faithful and constant, moderately addicted to its pleasures—he will be a kind, affectionate father, a good husband, a sincere friend, and of an industrious turn.

A woman born at the same time will be modest, chaste, good-tempered, cleanly in her habits, industrious, and charitable—in love she will be faithful, and in life she will be rather happy than otherwise, but be little concerned about wordly affairs—she will make an amiable mother, be decently fond of her husband, and moderately given to the joys of Hymen.

APRIL.—*Taurus, or the Bull.*

About the twentieth of the month the sun enters this sign: a man born at this time will be of a strong and robust constitution, faithful to his engagements, industrious, sober, and honest, but prone to anger—in life he will be ardent in his pursuits, but will meet with many vexations and disappointments—in love he will be extremely amorous, much given to women, of a jealous disposition, liable to infidelity to the marriage bed, but on the whole a good husband and a kind father—he will be extremely desirous of roving in the world, and establishing a reputation.

A woman born at this period will be of a courageous and resolute disposition, of an industrious turn, impatient of control, desirous of praise, and not easily daunted, fond of domestic life, much attached to those pleasures that are consistent with virtue, fond of her husband, indulgent to her children, and a sincere friend, and liberal benefactress—she will be happy in the connubial state, and pass her time with much satisfaction.

MAY.—*Gemini, or the Twins.*

About the twentieth of the month the sun enters this sign: a man born at this period will be of an undaunted courage, of a sweet and cheerful temper, of a lively imagination, stern in his resentments, though not easily provoked—he will be very ambitious of distinguishing himself for his learning and his knowledge of his profession or trade—in life he will be inclined to traveling, especially in foreign countries—he will meet with many crosses, and much persecution, but will bear them all with manly fortitude, and great patience—he will be immoderately attached to women, placing all his happiness in their arms—he will make a good father, but an unfaithful husband.

A woman born of this period will be of a peevish and fretful temper—she will be vindictive and revengeful, not very industrious, but inclined to neatness in dress and in her house—in love she will be credulous and jealous, much inclined to the pleasures of the marriage bed—in life she will meet with many disagreeable interruptions to her peace of mind, but be of a generous disposition, kind to her children, affectionate to her husband, and liberal to her dependents.

JUNE.—*Cancer, or the Crab.*

About the twentieth of the month the sun enters this sign; a man born at this period will be of an industrious and sober disposition, diffident of his own abilities, not easily excited to mirth, firm and inflexible in his determinations—in life, he will be faithful to his engagements, successful in his pursuits, and kind to his fellow-creatures—in love he will be sincere, moderately inclined to the joys of Hymen, faithful to the nuptial bed, a tender father, and a kind husband.

A woman born at this time will be of a captious temper, inclined to industry, and fond of merriment and good cheer—in life she will be persevering in her undertakings, tenacious of her own opinion, but without provoking obstinacy—she will be much inclined to the pleasures of love in a lawful manner, will make a good wife and an affectionate mother, and enjoy a reasonable share of happiness and tranquillity.

JULY.—*Leo, or the Lion.*

About the twentieth of the month the sun enters this sign: a man born at this period will be of an unruly, turbulent, rapacious, and quarrelsome disposition, always inclined to dispute with his neighbors, and enter into lawsuits—in life he will be forever scheming, without accomplishing his ends; he will be troublesome to others and to himself, and for the most part be unhappy—in love he will be indifferent, making it a secondary consideration—he will be unfaithful whenever is interests so dictate—he will make a morose husband, and negligent father.

A woman born at this time will be of an abusive and quarrelsome disposition, indolent and peevish in her temper, fond of calumniating her neighbors—she will be little inclined to the pleasures of love, be a very indifferent mother, and a sluttish wife—in life she will be perpetually in scrapes, and be for the most part unhappy herself by endeavoring   make others so.

AUGUST.—*Virgo, or the Virgin.*

About the twentieth of the month the sun enters this sign: a man born at this period will be of rather a timid disposition, though not cowardly—he will be honest and sincere in his dealings, much reserved in conversation, cautious in his undertakings, good-tempered and mild, gentle in his behavior, and sober in his conduct—in life he will be tolerably happy and moderately successful—in love he will be much inclined to lawless pleasures, yet affectionate to his wife—he will make a good father and a tender husband.

A woman born at this time will be of a very honest, sincere, and candid disposition, much inclined to cleanliness in her person, of warm desires, modest speech, fond of connubial joys, and faithful to her husband—she will make a good mother and an industrious wife.

SEPTEMBER.—*Libra, or the balance.*

About the twentieth of the month the sun enters this sign: a man born at this period will be of an honest, sober, and upright disposition, faithful and just in his dealings, a great lover of truth, and an enemy to quarrels and disturbances—in life he will be highly respected, whatever may be his situation, rich or poor—if he arrives at honors and places of consequence, he will still retain a veneration for his old friends, protect them to the utmost of his power, and conduct himself with temper and moderation—in love he will be no enemy to the pleasures of wedlock, but make an affectionate husband and kind father.

A woman born at this time will be of a prudent, modest, and virtuous disposition, dignified in her manners, affable and agreeable in her conversation, generous in her temper, in life she will be very happy—in the business of love she will only consider it as a duty in obedience to her husband, and will make an obedient and complying wife, and a careful and attentive mother.

OCTOBER.—*Scorpio, or the Scorpion.*

About the twentieth of the month the sun enters this sign: a man born at this period will be of an amiable and social disposition, of a lively imagination, prudent in his conduct, and agreeable in his manners. In life he will be subject to many cruel and severe hardships, he will have many enemies, be suspected of plots and conspiracies against the state; he will be persecuted and calumniated, but by the interposition of friends he will be raised by his merits, in the end triumph over his enemies, and be extricated from his difficulties. In love he will be faithful and sincere, much addicted to the delights of the connubial state, but obliged to make his passions yield to his other concerns in life; he will be a fond father and an affectionate husband.

A woman born at this time will be of a rash, imperious, intriguing, and designing disposition, of an unsteady and disagreeable temper, and inclined to liquor. In life her schemes will generally miscarry through her own folly and want of conduct. In love she will yield to its pleasures only with a view to serve her purpose, and she will be fickle and unfaithful—make a bad wife, savage mother, and be the cause of her family's unhappiness.

NOVEMBER.—*Sagittarius, or the Archer.*

About the twentieth of the month the sun enters this sign: a man born at this period will be of a cold, phlegmatic disposition, of little sensibility, furious when in a passion, implacable in his resentments, punctual in his dealings. In life he will be generally successful, easily led by others, and frequently deceived. In love he will be moderate in his passions, caressing his wife merely for the sake of getting children, to whom he will make an excellent father, but will be a morose and tyrannical husband.

A woman born at this time will be of a masculine disposition, much addicted to calumniate others, and spreading scandalous reports of those she does not like: in her behavior she will be imperious and disagreeable, a great scold, and inclined to strong liquors and quarreling. In life she will make many enemies by her want of conduct and little regard to what she says, be rather unhappy and unsuccessful in her pursuits. In love she will be constant, but expect to govern her husband—she will expect him to do strict justice to the marriage-bed, to the pleasures of which she will be immoderately attached; she will love her children but be negligent of them; she will be fond of her husband whilst he gives her her own way, and strictly performs the marriage rites; but if they are neglected, she will lead him a wearisome life, and prove unfaithful.

DECEMBER.—*Capricorn, or the Horned Goat.*

About the twentieth of the month the sun enters this sign: a man born at this time will be of an ambitious, turbulent, and restless disposition, troublesome to himself and others, of a dull and lazy habit, void of reflection, and of unpleasant manners. In life he will be unhappy and unfortunate, owing to his own rashness and want of consideration. In love he will be exceedingly amorous, much attached to the female sex, rather fickle in his affections, but kind and loving to his wife, punctual in the discharge of the nuptial duties; he will make a bad father, but a good husband.

A woman born at this time will be of a meek, sober, and amiable disposition, a good neighbor and a sincere friend, fearful and timorous, but of engaging manners. In life she will be rather happy than otherwise, and easily restrained from doing wrong. In love she will be of a warm constitution, and yield easily to the solicitations of her lovers; in the married state she will be faithful and kind, strongly attached to the hymenial duties, and forward in exacting them of her husband; she will be a tender mother and a good wife, though extremely credulous of everything she hears.

CURIOUS GAMES WITH CARDS.

By which fortunes are told in a singular and most diverting manner.

LOVERS' HEARTS.

FOUR young persons, but not more, may play at this game; or three, by making a dumb hand, or sleeping partner, as at whist. Play this game exactly the same in every game, making the queen, whom you call Venus, above ace, the aces in this game only standing for one, and hearts must be first led off by the person next the dealer. He or she who gets most tricks this way (each taking up their own, and no partnership) will have most lovers, and the king and queen of hearts in one hand shows matrimony at hand; but woe to the unlucky one that gets no tricks at the deal, or does not hold a heart in their hand, they will be unfortunate in love, and long tarry before they marry.

CUPID AND HYMEN.

Three are enough for this game, the nines, the threes, and the aces; deal them equally; those who hold kings. hold friends; queens are rivals; knaves, shame; knave alone, lover; three, surprises; ace, sorrow; two together, shows a child before marriage; if a king alone is in her hand with the aces, she stands a good chance; but if a queen is with him, she will never marry the father; the nine of hearts gives the wish that you have most at heart; the nine of diamonds, money; and the nine of clubs, a new gown or coat; but the nine of spades is sorrow. A queen and a knave in one hand, bids fair for a secret intrigue.

HYMEN'S LOTTERY.

Let each one present deposit any sum agreed on, but of course some trifle; put a complete pack of cards, well shuffled, in a bag or reticule. Let the party stand in a circle, and the bag being handed around, each draw three. Pairs of any are favorable omens of some good fortune about to occur to the party, and gets from the pool the sum back each agreed to pay. The king of hearts is here made the god of love, and claims double, and gives a faithful swain to the fair one who has the good fortune to draw him; if Venus, the queen of hearts, is with him, it is the conquering prize, and clears the pool; fives and nines are reckoned crosses and misfortunes, and pay a forfeit of the sum agreed on to the pool, besides the usual stipend at each new game; three nines at one draw shows the lady will be an old maid; three fives a bad husband.

MATRIMONY.

Let three, five or seven young women stand in a circle, and draw a card out of a bag; she who gets the highest card out, will be married first of the company, whether she be at the present time maid, wife, or widow; and she who has the lowest has the longest time to stay ere the sun shines on her wedding-day; she who draws the ace of spades will never bear the name of wife; and she who has the nine of hearts in this trial will have one lover too many to her sorrow.

CUPID'S PASTIME.

By this game you may amuse yourself and friends, and at the same time learn some curious particulars of your future fate; and though apparently a simple, yet it is a sure method, as several young persons have acknowleged to the sibyl who first presented them with the rules.

Several may play at the game, it requiring no number, on

leaving out nine on their board, not exposed to view; each person puts a half-penny in the pool, and the dealer double. The ace of diamonds is made principal, and takes all the other aces, etc., like Pam at Loo; twos and threes in your hand are luck; four, a continuance in your present state; fives, trouble; sixes, profit; sevens, plague; eights, disappointments; nines, surprises; tens, settlement; knaves, sweethearts; kings and queens, friends and acquaintances; ace of spades, death; ace of clubs, a letter; and the ace of diamonds, with the ten of hearts, marriage.

The ace of diamonds being played first, or if it be not cut, the dealer calls for the queen of hearts, which takes next; if the ace be not cut, and the queen conquers, the person who played her will marry that year without a doubt, though it may perhaps seem unluckily at the time; but if she loses her queen, she must wait longer; the ace and queen being called, the rest go in rotation, as at whist, kings taking queens, queens knaves, and so on, and the more tricks you have, the more money you get off the board on the division of each game; those who hold the nine of spades will soon have some trouble, and they are also to pay a penny to the board; but the fortunate fair one who holds the queen and knave of hearts in the same hand will soon be married; or, if she is already within the pale of matrimony, she will have a great rise in life by means of her husband; those who hold the ace of diamonds and queen of hearts, clear the money off the board, and end that game; it also betokens great prosperity.

DICE.

This is a certain and innocent way of finding out common occurrences about to take place. Take three dice, shake them well in the box with your left hand, and then cast them out on a board or table, on which you had previously drawn a circle with chalk, but never throw on Monday or Wednesday.

Three—a pleasing surprise.

Four—a disagreeable one.

Five—a stranger who will prove a friend.

Six—loss of property.

Seven—undeserved scandal.

Eight—merited reproach.

Nine—a wedding.

Ten—a christening, at which some important event will occur to you.

Eleven—a death that concerns you.

Twelve—a letter speedily.

Thirteen—tears and sighs.

Fourteen—a new admirer.

Fifteen—beware that you are not drawn into some trouble or plot.

Sixteen—a pleasant journey.

Seventeen—you will either be on the water, or have dealing with those belonging to it, to your advantage.

Eighteen—a great profit, rise in life, or some most desirable good will happen almost immediately; for the answers to the dice are always fulfilled within nine days. To show the same number twice at one trial, shows news from abroad, be the number what they may. If the dice roll over the circle, the number thrown goes for nothing, but the occurrence shows sharp words, and if they fall to the floor it is blows, in throwing out the dice, if one remains on the top of the other. it is a present, of which I would have the females beware.

DOMINOES.

Lay them with their faces on the table, and shuffle them; then draw one, and see the number. N. B.—Never play on a Friday.

Double-six—receiving a handsome sum of money.

Six-five—going to a public amusement..

Six-four—lawsuits.

Six-three—ride in a coach.

Six-two—present of clothing.

Six-one—you will soon perform a friendly action.

Six-blank—guard against scandal, or you will suffer by your inattention.

Double-five—a new abode to your advantage.

Five-four—a fortunate speculation.

Five-three—a visit from a superior.

Five-two—a water-party.

Five-one—a love intrigue.

Five-blank—a funeral, but not of a relation.

Double-four—drinking liquor at a distance.

Four-three—a false alarm at your house.

Four-two—beware of thieves or swindlers.—Ladies, take notice of this; it means more than it says.

Four-one—trouble from creditors.

Four-blank—receive a letter from an angry friend.

Double-three—sudden wedding, at which you will be vexed.

Three-two—buy no lottery tickets, nor enter into any game of chance, or you will lose.

Three-one—a great discovery at hand.

Three-blank—an illegitimate child.

Double-two—you will be plagued by a jealous partner.

Two-one—you will mortgage or pledge some property very soon.

Double-one—you will soon find something to your advantage in the street or road.

Double-blank—the worst presage in all the set of dominoes: you will soon meet trouble from a quarter for which you are quite unprepared.

It is useless for any person to draw more than three dominoes at one time of trial, or in one and the same month, as they will only deceive themselves; shuffle the dominoes each time of choosing; to draw the same domino twice makes the answer stronger.

THE ART OF FORETELLING FUTURE EVENTS BY CHARMS, SPELLS, AND INCANTATIONS.

Magic Laurel.

Rise between three and four in the morning of your birthday, with cautious secrecy, so as to be observed by no one, and pluck a sprig of laurel; convey it to your chamber, and hold it over some lighted brimstone for five minutes, which you must carefully note by a watch or dial; wrap it in a white linen cloth or napkin, together with your own name written on writing-paper, and that of the young man who addresses you (or if there is more than one, write all the names down); write also the day of the week, the date of the year, and the age of the moon; then haste and bury it in the ground, where you will be sure it will not be disturbed for three days and three nights; then take it up and place the parcel under your pillow for three nights, and your dreams will be truly prophetic as to your destiny.

The Three Keys.

Purchase three small keys, each at a different place, and going to bed tie them together with your garter, and place them in your left-hand glove, along with a small flat dough-cake, on which you have pricked the first letters of your sweetheart's name; put them in your bosom when you retire to rest; if you are to have that young man you will dream of him, but not else.

This charm is the most effectual on the first or third of a new moon.

The Card Charm.

Select all the hearts and diamonds from the pack, put them in one of your stockings, and place them under your pillow any Friday night; as soon as you wake on Saturday morning, provided the fourth hour has struck, not else, draw a card: according to the number of pips, so many years will elapse before you appear at the altar of Hymen. Hearts show a loving husband, diamonds the richest husband or wife; the kings show that you will never marry; the queen, a troublesome rival; the knave of diamonds, a fatal seduction; and the knave of hearts, early widowhood.

The Magic Ring.

Borrow a wedding-ring concealing the purpose for which you borrow it; but no widow's or pretended marriage will do; it spoils the charm; wear it for three hours at least before you retire to rest, and then suspend it by a hair off your head over your pillow; write within a circle resembling a ring, the sentence from the matrimonial service, beginning with, *with this ring I thee wed*, and over the circle write your own name in full length, and the figures that stand for your age; place it under your pillow, and your dream will fully explain who you are to marry, and what kind of a fate you will have with them. If your dream is too confused to remember it, or you do not dream at all, it is a certain sign you will never be a bride.

The Witches' Chain.

Let three young women join in making a long chain, about a yard will do, of Christmas juniper and misletoe berries, and at the end of every link put an oak acorn. Exactly before midnight let them assemble in a room by themselves, where no one can disturb them; leave a window open, and take the key out of the key-hole and hang it over the chimney-piece; have a good fire and place in the midst of it a long, thinnish log of wood, well sprinkled with oil, salt and fresh mold, then wrap the chain around it, each maiden having an equal share in the business; then sit down, and on your left knee let each fair one have a prayer-book opened at the matrimonial service. Just as the last acorn is burnt, the future husband will cross the room; each one will see her own proper spouse; but he will be invisible to the rest of the wakeful virgins. Those that are not to wed will see a coffin, or some misshapen form, cross the room; go to bed instantly and you will have remarkable dreams. This must be done either on a Wednesday or Friday night, but no other.

The Nine Keys.

Get nine small keys, they must all be your own by begging or purchase (borrowing will not do, nor must you tell what you want them for); plait a three-plaited band of your own hair, and tie them together, fastening the ends with nine knots: fasten them with one of your garters to your left wrist on going to bed, and bind the other garter round your head; then say:

> St. Peter take it not amiss,
> To try your favor I've done this;
> You are the ruler of the keys,
> Favor me then, if you please;
> Let me then your influence prove,
> And see my dear and wedded love!

This must be done on the eve of St. Peter's, and is an old charm used by the maidens of Rome in ancient time, who put great faith in it.

The Mysterious Watch.

Request any person to lend you his watch, and ask him if it will go when laid on the table.   He will, no doubt, answer in the affirmative; in which case place it over the end of the concealed magnet, and it will presently stop.   Then mark the precise spot where you placed the watch, and moving the point of the magnet, give the watch to another person, and desire him to make the experiment; in which he, not succeeding, gives it to a third (at the same time replacing the magnet), and he will immediately perform it, to the great chagrin of the second party.

This experiment cannot be effected unless you take the precaution to use a very strongly impregnated magnetic bar, and that the balance-wheel of the watch be of steel, which may be ascertained by previously opening it, and looking -at the works.

St. Agnes' Day—Charm to know who your husband shall be.

Falls on the 21st of January; you must prepare yourself by a twenty-four hour' fast, touching nothing but pure spring water, beginning at midnight on the 20th to the same again on the 21st; then go to bed, and mind you sleep by yourself, and do not mention what you are trying to any one, or it will break the spell; go to rest on your left side, and repeat these lines three times—

> St. Agnes be a friend to me,
> In the gift I ask of thee;
> Let me this night my husband see—

and you will dream of your future spouse; if you see more than one in your dream, you will wed two or three times, but if you sleep and dream not, you will never marry.

THE END.

HISTORICAL WORKS.

Famous Heroes and Heroines of History,

WITH NARRATIVES OF THEIR

MOST STIRRING ADVENTURES ON LAND AND SEA,

TOGETHER WITH DESCRIPTIONS OF THE

Great Battle-Fields of the World, Naval Engagements, and Noted Sieges. Price 25 cents.

For sale by all newsdealers in the United States and Canada, or sent to your address, post-paid, on receipt of the price. Address

FRANK TOUSEY, Publisher,
Box 2730. 34 and 36 North Moore Street, New York.

Loves and Intrigues of Kings and Queens,

Embracing the Romantic Adventures of the most remarkable

Heroes, Rulers, Statesmen, and Prelates,

who have figured in the History of the World, as well as the Amours of

THE GREAT EMPRESSES, QUEENS, AND PRINCESSES.

Price 25 cents. For sale by all newsdealers in the United States and Canada, or sent to your address, post-paid, on receipt of price. Address **FRANK TOUSEY, Publisher,**
Box 2730. 34 and 36 North Moore Street, New York.

Famous Assassinations of History,

From the time of Julius Cæsar to the present day, embracing the

LOVES, ADVENTURES, AND REVENGES

of many of the great characters who have figured conspicuously in the dramas of the world. Also containing the lives and tragic deaths of the noted American assassins,

John Wilkes Booth and Charles J. Guiteau,

together with a full account of the MYSTERIOUS ASSASSINATIONS IN PHENIX PARK, DUBLIN. Price 25 cents. For sale by all newsdealers in the United States and Canada, or sent to your address, postpaid, on receipt of price. Address

FRANK TOUSEY, Publisher,
Box 2730. 34 and 36 North Moore Street, New York.

Popular Songs and Ballads OF THE Emerald Isle

The grandest collection of IRISH POEMS AND SONGS ever offered to the public. The most popular effusions of Moore, T. Davis, Griffin, Lover, Mangan, Walsh, Callanan, Banim, Kickham, F. Davis, Goldsmith, Lever, Duffy, Casey, Meagher, Sullivan, O'Reilly, Locke, Meany, McCarthy, Mulchinock, Savage, Doheny, with sketches of their lives. The book is beautifully bound, and should be in the parlor of every family. For sale by all newsdealers. Price 25 cents. Sent, postpaid, on receipt of price. Address

FRANK TOUSEY, Publisher,
Box 2730. 34 and 36 North Moore Street, New York.